P9-DDY-726

DATE DUE

Frog and Friends

Celebrate Thanksgiving, Christmas, and New Year's Eve

Hudson Library
PO Box 401
Hudson, IL 61748

3.99 - Replacement

Written by Eve Bunting

Illustrated by Josée Masse

See other books in our I Am A Reader! series

To Keelin, who loves to read about Frog and his friends
—*Eve*

To my families: the Masses, the Plantes, and the Normandins
—*Josée*

This book has a reading comprehension level of 2.5 under the ATOS® readability formula.
For information about ATOS please visit www.renlearn.com.
ATOS is a registered trademark of Renaissance Learning, Inc.

Lexile®, Lexile® Framework and the Lexile® logo are trademarks of MetaMetrics, Inc.,
and are registered in the United States and abroad. The trademarks and names of other
companies and products mentioned herein are the property of their respective owners.
Copyright © 2010 MetaMetrics, Inc. All rights reserved.

Text Copyright © 2015 Eve Bunting
Illustration Copyright © 2015 Josée Masse

All rights reserved. No part of this book may be reproduced in any manner
without the express written consent of the publisher, except in the case of brief
excerpts in critical reviews and articles. All inquiries should be addressed to:

Sleeping Bear Press™

2395 South Huron Parkway, Suite 200
Ann Arbor, MI 48104
www.sleepingbearpress.com

Printed and bound in the United States.

10 9 8 7 6 5 4 3 2 1 (case)
10 9 8 7 6 5 4 3 2 1 (pbk)

Bunting, Eve, 1928- • Frog and friends : celebrate Thanksgiving, Christmas, and New Year's Eve / written by Eve Bunting; • illustrated by Josée Masse. • pages cm • Summary: "A beginning reader book containing three stories in which Frog shares a Thanksgiving feast with his woodland friends, celebrates his first Christmas, and rings in the New Year with a twist on tradition"–Provided by publisher. • ISBN 978-1-58536-897-6 (hard cover) – ISBN 978-1-58536-933-1 (paper back) • [1. Frogs–Fiction. 2. Animals–Fiction. 3. Friendship–Fiction. 4. Thanksgiving Day–Fiction. 5. Christmas–Fiction. 6. New Year–Fiction.] I. Masse, Josée, illustrator. II. Title. III. Title: Celebrate Thanksgiving, Christmas, and New Year's Eve. • PZ7.B91527Fsc 2015 • [E]–dc23 • 2015003429

Table of Contents

Hudson Area Public Library
PO 461
Hudson, IL 61748

DISCARD

Thanksgiving

Frog and his friends loved Thanksgiving.

They invited everyone they knew. And even those they did not know.

"It is a time of love. And sharing," Frog said.

They had a big, big table.

It was the stump of a big, big tree.

They always thanked the tree's roots for letting them use it.

The birds came, and the crickets.

Rabbit's children, old and new, came.

There were so many of them they had to sit on the grass.

Hippo came late.

"I had Thanksgiving dinner at the Little

Zoo," he said. "But I am hungry again."

The Thanksgiving meal was always a

treat. Flies, mealworms, caterpillars, ants.

Kale and wild mushroom salad with

watercress dressing.

They had ferns and soft grass for Hippo.

To begin they held paws and feet and claws.

Then Frog stood. He gave thanks for friends and for happy lives.

They were just about to eat when a little voice said, "Hello!"

"What? Who?"

Frog looked and saw a tiny hedgehog.

"Hello," he called back. "Do you want to come eat with us?"

"Yes, please," the tiny hedgehog said. "I am on my way to my grandmother's house. I am hungry."

"Come," Frog said kindly. "May we call you Hedgie?"

Hedgie nodded. She came closer.

Then she saw Hippo.

Suddenly her quills went up.

She curled into a spiky ball.

Only her head stuck out.

Possum screamed.

Squirrel scampered to the top of a tree.

Raccoon poked one of the hedgehog's quills and yelled, "Ow! Sharp!"

"Little Possums," Possum called. "Come to Mama. Do not go near the hedgehog!"

"It is all right," Frog said. "Hedgie puts out her quills when she is scared. Her quills keep her safe."

Hedgie was looking at Hippo.

"I am scared of him," she said. "He is so big. He has a big mouth. He could eat a little hedgehog."

Hippo came close to her. "I will not hurt you," he said.

"Hippo is our friend," Frog told her. "He is kind and gentle."

"I am, too." Hedgie whispered. She put her quills down. "See?"

They all moved closer to her.

"You have nice eyes," Squirrel told her.

"I like your nose," Rabbit said.

Hippo smiled at Hedgie. "When you are big like me, or spiky like you, everyone is scared. Till they get to know you. Come sit by me," he told her.

"We are glad to have you, Hedgie," Frog said.

"May I also take a doggie bag for my grandmother?" Hedgie asked.

"Yes," Frog said. "There is lots of food."

He looked around the table.

"I love you all," he said. "Happy Thanksgiving."

The Christmas Tree

"Usually I am asleep at Christmas," Frog said. "I hibernate. But I would like to be awake this Christmas. It sounds like fun. Will you waken me?"

Little Jumping Mouse clapped her paws. "Of course. Last year I was alone at Christmas. It was not so merry. But now I have friends." She blew kisses all around.

"Will you tell us about Christmas trees, Jumping Mouse?" Raccoon asked. "I have heard of them."

Little Jumping Mouse perked up her ears. She liked to be asked.

Frog and Raccoon and Squirrel and Possum and Rabbit and Chameleon felt lucky to have her for a friend. Little Jumping Mouse knew a lot.

"It is not because I am smarter," she said modestly. "It is because I am a mouse. I am small. I can go into houses. I can listen and see and smell. I can smell chocolate from a long way away." She licked her lips.

"What is chocolate?" Squirrel asked.

"It is …" little Jumping Mouse began.

"Can we talk about the Christmas tree?" Frog asked.

"It is a tree you find in the woods," Jumping Mouse told them. "At Christmas you bring it into your house."

Raccoon looked worried. "We do not have a house big enough for a tree."

"But we have trees all around Frog's pond," Jumping Mouse said. "It does not have to be big. Small is better. We can have an outside Christmas tree."

Possum clapped her paws. Her babies shouted, "Yippee! Yippee!"

Frog yawned. "I will sleep till it is time,"

he said.

On the day before Christmas they
wakened him.

Together they chose the perfect tree.

Frog stretched. "Now what do we do?"

He was still a little sleepy.

"We make the tree pretty," little Jumping Mouse told them.

"Everyone come tonight. Bring something pretty to hang on our tree," Frog said.

Chameleon ran to pet the tree and turned a lovely shade of green.

"I feel like Christmas already," he said.

That night they met by their tree.

Squirrel brought a chain of acorns he

had strung. He hung it on a branch.

"Lovely," his friends said.

Possum brought some red knitted balls

she and one of her little possums had made.

"Lovely," her friends said.

Raccoon brought an orange she had

taken from Mr. Black's yard.

"Lovely," they all said.

"We can share it after Christmas,"

Raccoon told them.

Little Jumping Mouse brought something that was flat and golden.

"It is a square of chocolate," she said. "It is covered with gold paper. We can share it too, after Christmas."

Chameleon brought red berries from a holly bush.

Rabbit brought a bright orange carrot with a ferny top.

"Lovely," they said.

Frog brought the lid of an empty can. "Someone threw it away," he said.

It shone silver in the moonlight.

"Lovely," they told him.

Then they lay on their bellies around

their tree.

"There is one thing missing," little Jumping Mouse said. "There must always be a star on top of a Christmas tree."

"Oh dear! Oh no!"

"Wait!" Frog pointed up.

In the sky, below the moon, a star hung. It was right above their tree.

"So lovely. So lovely," they whispered.

Then they all stood and held hands and sang "Old MacDonald Had a Farm" while the night and the moon and the Christmas star listened.

New Year's Eve

Frog and his friends were playing a game of tag when little Jumping Mouse rushed over to them.

"I have news," she said.

Frog could tell she was excited. Her nose twitched. Her whiskers quivered.

"News?" Frog asked and he and his friends sat down to listen.

They loved Mouse news.

Little Jumping Mouse was good at slipping into people's houses.

She was good at listening. And telling.

She sat down next to Frog.

"Two girls were talking," Jumping Mouse said. "I listened. They said New Year's Day is tomorrow. And tonight is New Year's Eve. They said this is the best night of the whole year."

"Better than Christmas Eve?" Raccoon asked.

"Well, no. But almost as good," Jumping Mouse said. "Everybody wears a funny hat. At the sound of the big bell they toss their hats into the air. That is the start of the new year."

"I have heard that big bell," Frog said. "I

didn't know what it meant."

"On New Year's Eve they dance," Jumping Mouse went on. "They sing. They party. They listen for the bell."

The little possums jumped up and down and turned somersaults.

"Party! Party! Party!" they shouted.

Rabbit clapped her paws. "We all love parties."

Her babies joined in. "Yes, yes, yes."

"There's more," Jumping Mouse said.

"New Year's Day is fun, too. The old year is over. Everyone is happy."

Frog frowned. "Why? I liked the old year."

"Well, on New Year's Day you promise to change. You promise to be better," Jumping Mouse told them.

"What if we don't want to change?" Squirrel asked.

"I don't want to," Raccoon said. "I like me the way I am."

"We like you the way you are, too," Rabbit said.

"And I don't want to change," she added. "What if my little rabbits didn't know me anymore?"

The little rabbits began to cry, "Don't change, Mama. Don't."

"I won't," Rabbit said and pulled them close to her.

Frog and his friends looked at each other.

"Who wants to change?" Frog asked.

Not a single paw or claw or foot went up.

"Who wants their friends to change?"

Not a single paw or claw or foot went up.

Little Jumping Mouse hung her head. "I thought this would be good," she said.

"It is good," Frog said. "Super good. We like us the way we are. That makes us real, true friends."

They ran to hug each other.

"So," Frog said, "let's forget New Year's

Day. We don't have to do everything people do. Who would like to have a New Year's Eve–Nobody–Changes party?"

Every paw and claw and foot went up!

They were busy the rest of the day

making party hats.

At night they met again.

There were hats of all kinds. Leaf hats,

water-lily hats, tin-can hats, fern hats,

bird's-nest hats.

It was all lovely.

They played Ring-Around-the-Rosy.

Sometimes their hats fell off.

Squirrel lent his tin-can hat so they

could play Kick the Can.

They sang and danced the Hickity Poo

while the moonlight danced in the bare tree

branches.

When the big bell rang for New Year's
Day none of them heard it.

They lay curled together, the way real,
true friends do.

All of them content.

All of them fast asleep.